THE BIG YELLOW SCHOOL BUS

By Bernard Wiseman

Illustrated by
Ed Rodriguez

DISNEY PRESS
NEW YORK

FIRST EDITION

1 3 5 7 9 10 8 6 4 2

Library of Congress Catalog Card Number: 91-58787
ISBN: 1-56282-048-6 / 1-56282-226-8 (lib. bdg.)

Mickey said, “Look, Goofy.

The school bus is coming.”

Goofy yelled, “Hello, school bus!”

Mickey got on the school bus.
Goofy jumped on next.
His ears flopped
up and down.
The driver said, “Do not forget.
Put on your seat belt.”
“Put on my WHAT?” Goofy asked.

The bus started to go.

Mickey said, “Your SEAT BELT.”

The bus hit a bump.

Goofy’s ears

kept flopping up and down.

Goofy said,
"I did not hear you.
What did you say?"
Mickey said, "I said,
'Your SEAT BELT.'"
Goofy's ears
were still flopping.
Goofy asked, "Did you say
my SEED BELT?"

"No!" said Mickey.
"I did not say,
'Your SEED BELT.'
I said, 'Your SEAT BELT.'"
The bus stopped.
Donald got on.
"SEED BELT is spelled
S-E-E-D B-E-L-T,"
said Mickey.
"SEAT BELT is spelled..."
"Wait!" Donald yelled.

"I am learning to spell.

Let me spell SEAT BELT."

The driver said,

"First put on your seat belt.

Then spell it."

The bus started to go.
It hit another bump.
Goofy's ears flopped again.

Donald said,

“SEAT BELT is spelled S-E-E-T...”

Goofy’s ears were still flopping.

Goofy said, “I did not hear you!

What did you say?”

Donald said, "I said,
'SEAT BELT is spelled S-E-E-T...'"
"No," said Mickey.
"SEAT BELT is spelled..."
The bus stopped again.
Minnie got on.
"Wait!" Minnie yelled.

“I am learning to spell.
Let me spell SEAT BELT.”
The driver said,
“First put on your seat belt.
Then spell it.”

The bus started to go.

Minnie said,

"SEAT BELT is spelled..."

The driver honked the horn.

The horn was loud.

Mickey and Goofy and
Donald said,
“We did not hear you!
What did you say?”

The bus hit another bump.

Goofy's ears flopped again.

Minnie said, "I said,

'SEAT BELT is spelled...'"

Goofy shouted,

"I did not hear you!

What did you say?"

The bus stopped again.

Daisy got on.

Minnie said,

"SEAT BELT is spelled..."

"Wait!" Daisy yelled.

"I am learning to spell.

Let me spell SEAT BELT."

"No!" Minnie yelled.

"Let me spell SEAT BELT."

“No!” Daisy yelled.

“Let me spell SEAT BELT.”

Mickey said, “Stop, stop! Look....

“We are at the school.
You can all spell SEAT BELT
on the way home.”

SCHOOL

THE WAY HOME

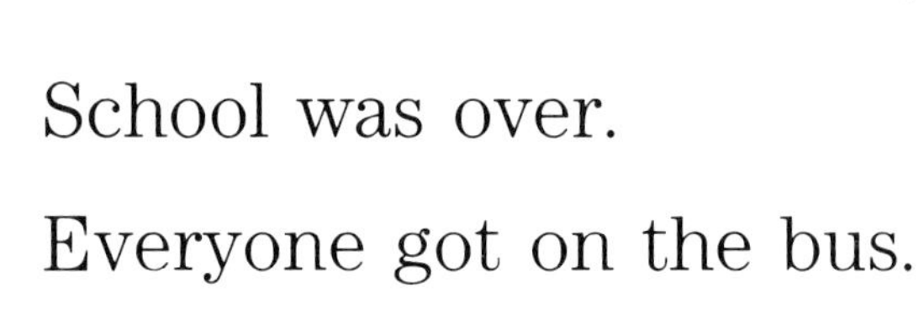

School was over.
Everyone got on the bus.
Daisy said,
“We are going home.
Now I will spell SEAT BELT.”
“No!” said Minnie.
“I will spell SEAT BELT!”
“Stop! Stop!” Mickey yelled.

The bus started to go.
It hit a bump.
Goofy's ears
flopped up and down.

Mickey waited for Goofy's ears
to stop flopping.
Then Mickey said,
"Let's do ARITHMETIC!
Daisy, pretend
you found ONE apple."

Daisy said,
"I am pretending
I found ONE apple."

Mickey said,
"Now pretend
you found another apple.
How many apples
would you have?"
Daisy said, "ONE."
"No!" said Mickey.
"You would have TWO."

The bus stopped.
As Daisy got off
she said, "ONE.

I would have only ONE apple.

I would eat

the first apple right away."

Minnie said,
"Arithmetic is fun!
Ask me arithmetic."
Mickey said, "Minnie, pretend
you found ONE penny."
Minnie said,
"I am pretending
I found ONE penny."

Mickey said,

"Now pretend

you found another penny.

You cannot eat pennies!

How many pennies

would you have?"

The bus stopped.
Minnie said, "NONE!
I would spend
the pennies right away."
Then she got off the bus.

The bus started again.

Donald said,

"Ask me arithmetic."

The bus hit a bump.

Goofy's ears

flopped up and down.

"Donald," said Mickey,

"pretend you found

ONE pebble."

Goofy cried,

“I did not hear you!

What did you say?”

"I said, 'Pretend
you found ONE pebble.'"
Goofy said,
"I am pretending
I found ONE pebble."

"No!" cried Donald.
"Mickey told ME
to pretend I found
ONE pebble!"

"Stop!" Mickey yelled.
"BOTH of you pretend
you found ONE pebble.
Now pretend you found
another pebble.
You cannot eat pebbles!
You cannot spend pebbles!
How many pebbles
would you have?"

The bus stopped.

Donald said, “NONE!

What good are pebbles?

I would throw them away.”

Then Donald got off.

The bus started to go.
Mickey asked Goofy,
"How many pebbles
would you have?"
Goofy said, "FOUR."

"FOUR?" said Mickey.

"You pretended

you found ONE pebble.

Then you pretended

you found another pebble.

How did you get FOUR?"

Goofy said,

“I like pebbles!

So I pretended

I kept my TWO pebbles.

And I pretended
I picked up
the TWO pebbles
Donald threw away."

The bus stopped one more time.
Mickey and Goofy got off.
Goofy said, "Tell me—how do
you spell SEAT BELT?"